Meddy Teddy woke up from his long winter's hibernation.
It was the first day of spring!

Meddy couldn't wait to go outside to explore. But Mama Teddy and Papa Teddy were still sleeping in their bed.

"I'll just go for a short walk and be back before they wake up,"
Meddy thought. He tiptoed out the front door.

Meddy paused in the warm morning sun.

"What a beautiful day!"

"Mama says the first thing I should do each day is greet the sun," Meddy said.

AHHHHHH...

Mountain Pose

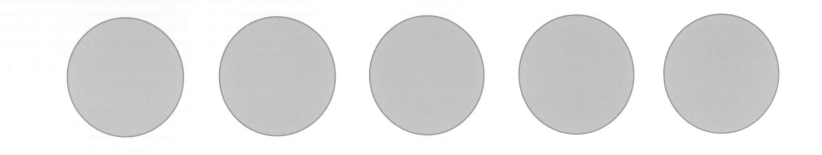

He took a deep breath and stood straight and tall.
Then he set off to enjoy the spring day.

Meddy hadn't walked very far when he ran into his friend Dog.

"Hi there," said Meddy. "Beautiful day for a walk, isn't it?"

"It certainly is," said Dog, excitedly running ahead.

Downward Dog

"Slow down, Dog," Meddy called after him. He bent down to smell some violets on the path. "If you go too fast, you'll miss the good things in life."

Dog stopped to smell the flowers, too. "Good idea, Meddy!" he said.

As Meddy made his way through the forest, he came upon his friend Beaver. She was busy working on her new lodge.

"I'm trying to put these twigs on top," said Beaver, "but I can't reach."

"Maybe I can help," said Meddy.

Tree Pose

Meddy reached as far as he could, stretching high on one leg. He was able to place the last sticks on top.

"Thank you, Meddy!" said Beaver.

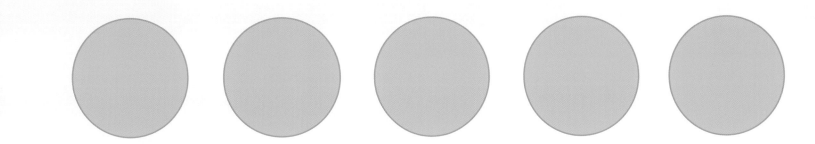

Meddy had walked a long way when he saw Frog sitting on a log.

"Hello, Frog," said Meddy. "What are you doing?"

"I'm listening to the breeze blowing by," said Frog.

Seated Twist

"Maybe if I sit like Frog, I can hear the breeze, too," thought Meddy. Together the two friends sat in silence.

When Meddy opened his eyes, he felt relaxed and quiet.

As Meddy walked through the forest, he paused to appreciate the budding trees and flowers.

Butterfly Pose

Meddy watched a butterfly fluttering by...

... and the clouds drifting slowly across the sky.

Meddy didn't want to miss a thing!

Happy Baby

Soon Meddy came upon his friend Hedgehog, who was sitting glumly on a stump.

"Why the long face?" asked Meddy.

Hedgehog was taking his own hike through the woods, but he had made a wrong turn and now he was lost.

"Do you remember anything on your walk that might help you find your way home?" asked Meddy. Hedgehog shook his head. Meddy could see his friend was worried.

"Let me show you what I do when I forget something," said Meddy. He kneeled on the ground with his arms stretched out in front of him. "Take a deep breath and focus on what you're trying to remember."

Hedgehog copied Meddy's pose. Then they both took a deep breath through their noses and let it out slowly.

Child's Pose

"I *do* remember something!" Hedgehog said excitedly. "I stopped to have lunch at a waterfall." He took out a map from his backpack and studied it with Meddy.

"There it is," said Meddy, finding the waterfall on the map. "And there's your house just beyond. When you find the waterfall, you'll be almost home."

Meddy lunged, then pointed Hedgehog in the right direction.

   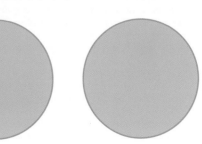

Crescent Lunge

Meddy realized it was time for him to go home, too. As he made
his way back, he passed Fox's den and stopped in to say hello.

"What are you up to?" Meddy asked Fox.

"I've been making fresh strawberry jam all day, but now I have to move all of these jars into my pantry," said Fox.

"Here, let me help," said Meddy, taking a jar and passing it to Fox.

Together the two friends worked until the job was done.

Warrior Two

Meddy continued on his journey and came upon Snake resting on a sunny rock.

"Hello, Meddy," said Snake. "Where are you off to?"

Meddy explained that he was on his way home. "I have to get back so my parents don't miss me when they wake up."

"I'm going in that direction," said Snake. "Why don't I join you?" The two friends made their way down the rocky path together.

Snake and Meddy came upon a fallen tree that was blocking the path. It was too big for Meddy to climb over.

Snake slithered easily underneath. "Follow me, Meddy," said Snake. "You can do it."

Meddy lay down on his stomach and wiggled under the tree.

"You're almost there!" said Snake encouragingly.

Meddy wiggled a little more, and then he was through.

Cobra Pose

As he made his way home, Meddy thought about the wonderful things he had seen on his journey— the birds, the butterflies, the flowers, and the trees.

And he thought about his many friends throughout the forest and how each one helped him appreciate this new spring day. Meddy felt peaceful.

When Meddy arrived home, Mama and Papa were still asleep in their bed. Meddy couldn't wait any longer.

"Mama! Papa! Wake up!" said Meddy.

Try all of the poses that

Meddy

**Mountain
Pose**

Downward Dog

**Butterfly
Pose**

Seated Twist

Tree Pose

Teddy

learned on his adventure!

Warrior Two

Happy Baby

Cobra Pose

Crescent Lunge

Child's Pose